School

The School Play

Willow and Sapphire practised together every second they could. Willow soon knew the whole script off by heart. However, Sapphire found it much harder to learn her lines, and as it got closer and closer to the performance, she got more and more nervous.

Linda Chapman lives in Leicestershire with her family and two Bernese mountain dogs. She used to be a stage manager in the theatre. When she is not writing she spends her time looking after her young family, horse riding and teaching drama. You can find out more about Linda on her website lindachapman.co.uk or visit mysecretunicorn.co.uk

Books by Linda Chapman

BRIGHT LIGHTS
CENTRE STAGE

MY SECRET UNICORN series

NOT QUITE A MERMAID series

STARDUST series

UNICORN SCHOOL series
(*Titles in reading order*)
FIRST CLASS FRIENDS
THE SURPRISE PARTY
THE TREASURE HUNT
THE SCHOOL PLAY

Unicorn School

The School Play

Linda Chapman

Illustrated by Ann Kronheimer

PUFFIN

PUFFIN BOOKS

Published by the Penguin Group
Penguin Books Ltd, 80 Strand, London WC2R ORL, England
Penguin Group (USA) Inc., 375 Hudson Street, New York, New York 10014, USA
Penguin Group (Canada), 90 Eglinton Avenue East, Suite 700, Toronto, Ontario, Canada M4P 2Y3
(a division of Pearson Penguin Canada Inc.)
Penguin Ireland, 25 St Stephen's Green, Dublin 2, Ireland (a division of Penguin Books Ltd)
Penguin Group (Australia), 250 Camberwell Road, Camberwell, Victoria 3124, Australia
(a division of Pearson Australia Group Pty Ltd)
Penguin Books India Pvt Ltd, 11 Community Centre, Panchsheel Park, New Delhi – 110 017, India
Penguin Group (NZ), 67 Apollo Drive, Rosedale, North Shore 0632, New Zealand
(a division of Pearson New Zealand Ltd)
Penguin Books (South Africa) (Pty) Ltd, 24 Sturdee Avenue, Rosebank, Johannesburg 2196, South Africa

Penguin Books Ltd, Registered Offices: 80 Strand, London WC2R ORL, England

puffinbooks.com

First published 2008
1

Text copyright © Working Partners Ltd, 2008
Illustrations copyright © Ann Kronheimer, 2008
All rights reserved

The moral right of the author and illustrator has been asserted

Set in Bembo
Typeset by Palimpsest Book Production Limited, Grangemouth, Stirlingshire
Made and printed in England by Clays Ltd, St Ives plc

British Library Cataloguing in Publication Data
A CIP catalogue record for this book is available from the British Library

ISBN: 978-0-141-32250-6

To Tahlia and Xanthe

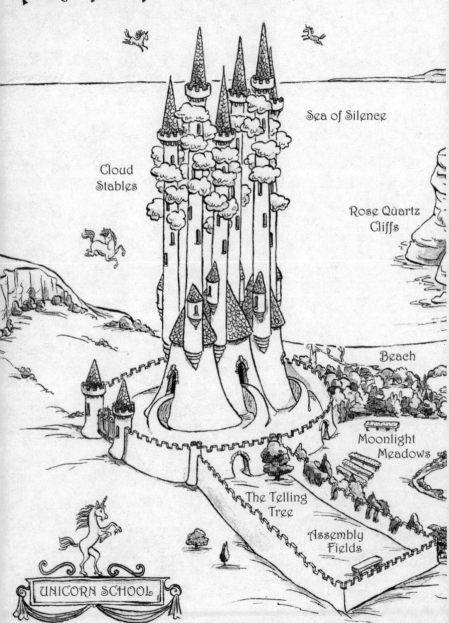

ARCADIA

Sea of Silence

Cloud
Stables

Rose Quartz
Cliffs

Beach

Moonlight
Meadows

The Telling
Tree

Assembly
Fields

UNICORN SCHOOL

High Winds Pass

Bramble Forest

Flying Heath

Charm Fields

N
W   E
S

Contents

An Important Announcement

'Come on, Willow, we don't want to be late for assembly!' Sapphire called.

Willow grabbed a last mouthful of sweet grass and then cantered across Moonlight Meadows to catch up with Sapphire, Storm and Troy, her three best friends. They joined the

crowd of other unicorns at Unicorn
School heading towards the
Assembly Fields. There was a buzz
of excited chatter in the air.

'I wonder what the announcement
is going to be about?' said Storm, a
very tall unicorn with a dark mane
and tail.

'I hope it's something exciting!' Willow said eagerly. The top of her head only came up to Storm's shoulder and she always felt tiny beside him.

Sapphire smiled and nudged Willow with her nose. 'You always want something exciting to happen, don't you?'

'Yep!' Willow agreed, tossing her mane.

'Perhaps there's going to be an extra flying race this month,' Troy suggested hopefully. He was an athletic, handsome unicorn who loved all sports and particularly flying.

'I hope there's going to be a

magic competition,' Storm put in. 'That would be fun!'

Willow plunged forward. 'Let's go and find out!'

The teachers were standing along one side of the Assembly Fields, making sure that everyone behaved and stood quietly.

As Willow joined the other Year One unicorns, there was the sound of a horn blowing, and three of the tall elves who helped in the school came marching into the field. The lead elf was blowing into a white conch shell. Behind him walked the other two elves and behind them came the Tricorn, the school's

Headmaster – a very wise-looking unicorn with a horn of three colours: gold, silver and bronze. He walked on to the stage and silence fell.

'Good morning, everyone,' the Tricorn said. 'As you know, today I have an important announcement to make.'

Willow and Sapphire exchanged excited looks.

'The teachers and I have decided that we should put on a school play,' said the Tricorn.

A breathless murmur ran round the listening unicorns.

'A play!' Willow whispered in delight. She loved acting.

'Oh, wow!' said Sapphire.

The Tricorn held his horn up and everyone immediately fell quiet. 'The play will be *Sleeping Beauty* and it is going to be performed on the last day of term when your parents come to collect you. Fern, our singing teacher, has offered to organize it. Tor, our transformation teacher, will be in charge of everything backstage – the costumes and the scenery. Any of you can audition to be in the play or volunteer to help Tor with the backstage tasks. Fern, would you now like to come and explain about the auditions?'

Fern, a plump, dapple-grey unicorn with a bronze horn, came out of the line of teachers and walked on to the stage. She was very jolly-looking and wore a purple scarf round her neck.

'Anyone who would like to act in the play must audition for a part,' she explained. 'To sign up you should go to the Telling Tree. There will be a piece of paper attached to it from morning break today. It lists all the acting parts in *Sleeping Beauty*. Just touch the name you would like to audition for with your horn. The Telling Tree will give you your audition time and a speech to learn. You will need to sing as well as act.'

The Tricorn stepped forward beside Fern. 'I wish you all the best of luck in the auditions. And now for the less exciting news. Rose-quartz-gazing club has had to be cancelled this lunchtime because of high tides. Also, the gusts on the High Winds Pass are too strong to have anyone risk going up there for racing and . . .'

Willow only vaguely heard the Tricorn reading out the rest of the day's notices. All she could think about was the play. She already knew she wanted to be Sleeping Beauty. Shutting her eyes, she imagined the hushed enjoyment of the audience as she sang a song. She imagined herself taking a bow at the end of the play and everyone saying she was the best Sleeping Beauty they had ever seen. She was just sighing happily when she suddenly felt someone's horn nudge into her neck. She jumped and blinked.

Troy grinned at her. 'Wakey-wakey, Willow! You can't fall asleep here!'

Willow realized that all the other

unicorns were moving off. Assembly had finished and she hadn't even noticed!

'I was thinking about the play.' Her dark eyes shone. 'Isn't it brilliant?'

'I can't see what all the fuss is about,' Troy shrugged. 'Who wants to act in some silly play? It would have been much more exciting if the Tricorn had announced a flying race.'

'You always want there to be flying races,' said Willow.

'That's because they're fun,' said Troy.

'Plays are much better!' Willow declared.

Sapphire and Storm nodded.

'I really want to help backstage,' said Storm. 'I'd love to make the scenery.'

'How about you, Sapphire?' Willow asked. Sapphire was very pretty with long dark eyelashes and a silken mane and tail, but she was also quite shy. 'Do you want to help backstage too?'

'Actually,' Sapphire said, 'I think I might like to audition.'

'Really?' Willow looked at her in surprise.

'I always act the main part if my brothers and sisters and I are putting on plays at home,' Sapphire admitted. 'I know that's just for our parents and I probably won't get a part in the school play but I'd still like to audition even though I'll be nervous.'

'Cool!' Willow said. It would be much more fun auditioning with Sapphire than on her own. 'Let's go to the Telling Tree at break time and sign up!'

'OK,' Sapphire grinned at her. 'Let's!'

Chapter Two

The Telling Tree

The sun was shining in the sky as Willow and her friends made their way to the Charm Fields for their first lesson of the day. Behind them the pearly-white turrets of the castle rose into the cornflower-blue sky. The unicorns at Unicorn School spent most of their time outside, but their bedrooms were in the clouds at the top of the six towers of the school. Willow swished her tail happily. She really enjoyed being at Unicorn School. She missed her mum and dad – and occasionally even missed her annoying older brothers – but she loved being at boarding school with all her friends and learning how to do magic.

'I wonder what we'll learn in transformation class today,' said Sapphire.

'Transformation is my favourite lesson,' Storm put in.

'That's because you're so good at it,' Willow told him.

In transformation classes they had to use their horns to turn objects from one thing into another.

'I'm not really,' Storm said modestly.

'Oh, yes you are!' Willow said.

Storm looked pleased but a bit embarrassed.

'Are you going to ask if you can help make the scenery for the play?' Sapphire said.

'Tor will probably want older unicorns, not a Year One like me,' said Storm.

'You should ask, anyway,' said Willow.

Tor was waiting for them. When all the Year Ones had arrived, he started the lesson. 'Today I am going to teach you how to use magic to transform leaves into plants,' he announced. 'To start, I will give you each three leaves from one of the magic oak trees that grow in Bramble Forest.'

Willow raised her horn to ask a question.

'Yes, Willow?'

'Why do we have to use leaves from a magic oak tree?' she asked curiously. 'Why can't we just use ordinary leaves?'

'To turn an ordinary leaf into something else needs very advanced magic,' Tor explained. 'It is much easier to use a leaf from a magic oak tree because it has magic in it already and will change into something else much more easily. Now who knows how to tell whether a leaf is from a magic oak tree or not?'

Storm put up his horn. 'Leaves

from a magic oak tree have all got a small golden dot where the stalk joins the leaf.'

'Correct,' said Tor approvingly. 'It is the same with any magical plant or any part of a magic tree – acorns, branches, roots all have a gold dot. Now let's begin. Look at the leaf on the floor and imagine a plant standing in its place. Think about all the details of the plant – the colour of its flowers, the size of it, the shape of its leaves – then touch your horn to the oak leaf and wait for your magic to work.'

Half an hour later, Willow was looking at a very limp plant with a purple flower that drooped on its long stem; Sapphire had a plant with small pink flowers that bent in one direction as if being blown by the wind; and Troy had a small weed.

Willow stared. 'Is that what you were imagining?'

'No,' Troy said ruefully. 'I was trying to imagine a sunflower.'

Willow giggled. 'I think you might need to work on your transformation skills, Troy!'

Troy grinned. 'Speak for yourself! Look what you managed to get!'

Willow giggled. She had to admit, he was right.

Troy glanced at Storm, who was

the only unicorn to have managed to transform all three of his leaves. The first leaf had become a small, neat plant with purple starry flowers all over; the second was a climbing bramble that had wound itself over a nearby tree stump; and the third was a neat rose bush. 'That's really good, Storm,' Troy said.

Tor came over, nodding approvingly. 'Excellent work, Storm! Would you be interested in helping with the scenery for the school play?'

'Really? Do you mean it? Well, yes!' Storm exclaimed.

'Good. I will be holding extra transformation classes for the unicorns who want to help. The first

will be on Sunday afternoon. I'll see
you there.'

And with that, Tor walked away.

Storm looked round at the others
in delight.

Willow grinned. 'I told you Tor
would want you to help.' She looked
at Sapphire. 'I hope we can get parts
in the play.'

'We should go to the Telling Tree

and sign up for the auditions,'
Sapphire said. 'Are you sure you
don't want to audition, Troy?'

'Absolutely positive,' Troy snorted.
'Come on, Storm. Let's go to the
meadows.'

Leaving Troy and Storm, Willow
and Sapphire set off towards the
Assembly Fields. The Telling Tree
stood at the opposite end to the stage.
It was a tall tree with an enormous
trunk and silvery-green leaves.

'There's the list!' said Sapphire,
pointing to a sheet of paper attached
to the broad trunk. There were
three other unicorns standing round
it. One of them was Oriel, a Year
Three.

'Hey, you two. Have you come to sign up?' he said. 'All the parts are listed here.' He pointed with his horn. Willow read down the list of characters' names and descriptions:

Sleeping Beauty – a shy, young, very beautiful character. A large acting and singing part.

The Wicked Fairy — a wicked character with a horrible laugh. Loud and scary. Some singing. The Prince — a handsome, strong, lively character. A medium acting and singing part. The King — a noble, wise, kindly character. No singing. The Queen — a noble, caring and loving character. No singing. The Fairy Godmothers — there will be eight fairy godmothers. Need to be able to fly well. Small singing parts.

And then there was a list of the smaller parts — animals in the woods and palace servants. Willow didn't

bother to read those. She didn't
want a small part!

'I'm going to audition to be the
Prince,' said Oriel. His horn
touched where it said *The Prince*
on the list. A shower of gold
sparks flew up into the sky. Willow
gasped and Sapphire jumped
backwards. Even Oriel started in
surprise. 'Whoa! Look what's
happening!'

In the air in front of him the
golden sparks met up and as they
came together they formed
shimmering golden words: Oriel.
The Prince. Saturday 10.00.

'That must be my audition time!'
As Oriel spoke, a piece of parchment

floated down from the leaves of the tree. They all stared at it.

'It's a speech from the play,' said Willow.

The golden sparks in the air formed a sentence: Learn this speech for the audition.

'Wow!' Oriel picked the paper up with his horn.

'I'm going to put my name down,' said Sapphire.

'What are you going to audition for?' Willow asked her.

Sapphire took a deep breath. 'I'm going to audition for . . .' Her horn touched the list. 'Sleeping Beauty!'

As the golden sparks shot out into the air, Willow looked at Sapphire in shock. She'd never imagined that her friend would audition for the main part.

Sapphire. Sleeping Beauty. Saturday 10.40, the words in gold said.

'But you said you'll be nervous and it's the main part, Sapphire!' Willow exclaimed.

'I know,' Sapphire replied, as a piece of paper fluttered down from the tree. 'I won't get it. I'm sure I'm nowhere near good enough. But it'll be fun to audition for it anyway.' She looked at Willow. 'Are you going to audition for Sleeping Beauty too?'

Willow hesitated. 'Well, I was

going to but . . .' She felt a bit odd.
She *wanted* to audition for Sleeping
Beauty but that would mean she
and Sapphire would be competing
against each other.

'But what?' Sapphire asked.

'Do you mind if I do?' Willow
said cautiously.

'Of course not!' said Sapphire. 'There'll be lots of other people trying out for the part too.'

Willow felt a rush of relief and quickly touched her horn to the list. A warm sparkly feeling seemed to run from her horn down to all four hooves. She blinked as the golden sparks shot into the air. *Willow. Sleeping Beauty. Saturday 10.30.*

Willow's audition speech floated down from the leaves of the Telling Tree. She picked it up. Excitement fizzed through her. 'We'd better get learning our lines!' she said. 'And fast!'

Chapter Three

Audition Time!

After supper, Willow and Sapphire found a quiet corner in Moonlight Meadows and practised their audition speeches. They each had the same one to learn. It was Sleeping Beauty on the morning of her sixteenth birthday, setting off to explore the castle.

'I wonder if one of us *will* get to be Sleeping Beauty,' Sapphire said when they finished practising and headed up to the stables.

'I hope so!' Willow said excitedly.

'I guess I don't really mind,' Sapphire said. 'It would be fun to be Sleeping Beauty but I'd also like to be one of the fairy godmothers or even just one of the woodland animals.'

But Willow didn't want to be an animal or a fairy godmother. *Oh, I hope I get to be Sleeping Beauty*, she thought.

On Saturday morning, they flew over to the Assembly Fields, where the auditions were taking place. When Willow and Sapphire got there, Oriel was in the middle of his audition for the Prince. He was standing on the platform and slashing his horn from side to side as if cutting through brambles. With a triumphant whinny, he came to the centre of the stage and began his speech.

'It is said that a beautiful princess lies in an enchanted sleep in a castle through these woods. I must get to her.' He began to sing:

'Through the woods I must go.
Through rain, hail, wind and snow.
I must cut the brambles tall
And reach the castle's stony wall.'

Oriel's voice was strong and clear.

'He's very good, isn't he?' Sapphire whispered.

Willow nodded. She couldn't wait for her chance to audition.

Sapphire fidgeted nervously. 'This is really scary. Maybe I shouldn't audition. Maybe I should pull out. Maybe –'

'You'll be fine!' Willow told her.

'Just do the speech like we've been practising it. You're really good, Sapphire.'

'Well done,' called Fern as Oriel finished. 'That was a really good audition, Oriel.'

Oriel looked pleased and left the stage.

'And now for the auditions for Sleeping Beauty,' announced Fern. 'We have five unicorns trying out for the part: Cadence, Meadowflax, Willow, Saffron and Sapphire. Cadence, could you come up onstage, please?'

Cadence, a pretty Year Three unicorn, walked on to the stage and began her audition. She had learnt

the same speech as Willow and
Sapphire but she spoke very softly
and they could hardly hear a word.

'She's much too quiet, isn't she?'
Willow whispered to Sapphire.

Cadence's singing was very good,
though, and Fern smiled at her
when she left the stage. 'Thank you,
Cadence.' She checked her list.
'Meadowflax, you're next.'

Meadowflax was a Year Two
unicorn with a long face. She
looked shy as she stood on
stage and she forgot her
lines four times.

'You're loads better than
either of them,' Sapphire
said to Willow. 'Good luck!'

Oh, please let me do OK, Willow thought.

Then Fern called Willow's name.

Willow trotted on to the stage. As soon as she looked out at the watching unicorns, confidence flooded through her. This was going to be fun! Speaking loudly and clearly, she began.

'It's my sixteenth birthday today. I wonder what I should do? Maybe I'll go exploring the castle . . .'

Willow got through her speech without one mistake and then sang the song.

'Excellent!' Fern said, smiling at her. 'That was a great audition, Willow!'

Willow trotted off the stage feeling very happy.

'Well done!' Sapphire whispered.

'Thanks,' said Willow.

They all fell silent as Saffron did her audition. Saffron spoke the words very stiffly.

'You were much better than her!' Sapphire whispered to Willow. 'In fact, you've easily been the best of everyone.' She looked nervous. 'It's my go next. I hope I do OK.'

'Good luck,' said Willow. As Sapphire went on to the stage, Willow started to imagine being Sleeping Beauty. She imagined a huge audience watching her. She imagined the whole show, the

cheering at the end of the
performance as she bowed . . .

Suddenly she blinked as she heard
Fern saying, 'Thank you, Sapphire.
That was a really good audition.'

'Whoops,' Willow muttered. She'd
been so lost in her daydreams that
she'd forgotten to watch Sapphire!

Sapphire trotted offstage. 'What
was I like?' she asked Willow eagerly.

'Really, really good,' Willow said, biting her bottom lip.

'I was so nervous at the beginning I was sure everyone could hear my voice shaking,' said Sapphire. 'But Fern seemed pleased so I guess I must have been OK. But nowhere near as good as you,' she added quickly. 'You were brilliant, Willow. I bet you get to be Sleeping Beauty.'

Willow grinned in delight.

Fern turned to them all. 'Thank you for auditioning. As you know, only one of you can be Sleeping Beauty. However, I will be considering the rest of you for other parts in the play. No one has put down to audition for the Wicked

Fairy and I need to choose all the fairy godmothers. I would like Cadence, Willow and Sapphire to come back for a second audition for Sleeping Beauty tomorrow, along with Topaz, Sorrel, Melody, Amethyst, Coral and Solitaire for the fairy godmothers' parts.

'We've got second auditions!' Sapphire exclaimed.

Willow tossed her head excitedly. So Sleeping Beauty would be either her or Sapphire or Cadence.

Oh, I hope it's me, she thought, *I really do!*

Chapter Four

Second Auditions

That afternoon, Willow wrote a letter home. Unicorns could write by using their horns. All they had to do was touch the paper with their horn and imagine what they wanted to write and the words appeared by magic. The letters they wrote were called emails – short for elfmails, because after they had written them the elves delivered them using elf magic.

Willow couldn't wait to tell her mum and dad all about the auditions. The more she thought about it, the more she believed that she really might get to be Sleeping Beauty. She quickly began to write.

Dear Mum and Dad,

I hope you are well. I am! We are doing a play of Sleeping Beauty *at school. I auditioned for it today and guess what? I think I am going to be Sleeping Beauty. Sapphire said I was really good at the audition. Fern said so too. We are doing the play at the end of term so you will be able to see me in it. Write soon!*

Lots of love,

Willow xxx

She picked up the note in her mouth and trotted into the castle. The elves who were in charge of the post worked in a large room just to the left of the front door. Willow knocked politely.

A voice called, 'Come in!'

Willow walked into the room. It had a high ceiling and large windows all the way round. A tall elf with pointed ears was sitting behind a desk beside one of the windows. Three more elves on the other side of the room were sorting the mail that had arrived into four piles.

'Yes?' the tall elf said to Willow. 'How may I help you?'

'I'd like to post this to my parents, please,' Willow said, giving him the letter.

'What are their names?' the elf asked.

'Stardust and Midnight,' Willow told him.

The elf addressed an envelope with a large quill dipped in magic purple elf ink. As he carefully wrote the names, Willow looked out of the window. She noticed that the lower branches of an oak tree were almost covering the glass. *A magic oak tree*, she thought as she realized that each leaf had a gold spot at its base.

The elf sealed the envelope. 'Right, it's ready to go,' he said. 'Touch it with your horn, please, Willow.'

Willow did as she was told and then the elf clapped his hands twice. The letter flew up into the air, spun around twice and disappeared with a faint pop.

'All done,' the elf declared. 'Your

parents should receive it tomorrow.'

Willow left the office. She wondered what her parents would say when they got the letter. They would be so proud if she got to be Sleeping Beauty.

You will, a little voice in her head said. *You know you will!*

The next morning, Willow and Sapphire went to the second auditions. These auditions were quite different from those of the day before. First Fern described a scene to them where Sleeping Beauty was exploring the castle and they had to take it in turns to act it out, making up the lines. Then they had to get into pairs and read a scene where the Wicked Fairy was trying to trick Sleeping Beauty into using the spinning wheel.

Fern and Cadence went as one pair, and Willow and Sapphire went together. Willow really enjoyed being the bad fairy. She stomped around the stage and tossed her mane and even made silver stars fly into the air when she was trying to get Sapphire to use the spinning wheel.

'Fantastic!' Fern cried. 'Oh, well done, Willow! Now let me see if you are just as good at being Sleeping Beauty.'

Willow and Sapphire swapped parts.

'That was wonderful!' Fern praised them as they finished the scene for the second time. 'You were a lovely Sleeping Beauty, Willow.'

Willow glowed.

Finally, Fern got Cadence, Willow and Sapphire to perform the speech they had learnt for the first audition all over again.

Willow spoke as loudly and as confidently as she could. Fern congratulated her when she had finished.

Willow trotted off the stage and Sapphire walked on. Willow watched closely. She wasn't going to miss Sapphire doing her speech again!

Sapphire stood timidly at the centre of the stage. She blinked her long eyelashes and began to speak. Her voice wasn't very loud but it was clear, and although she didn't look too confident, her slight air of shyness and nervousness seemed to suit the part of Sleeping Beauty.

'You were great,' Willow complimented Sapphire afterwards.

'Thanks,' Sapphire smiled. 'I was really nervous but I did enjoy it.'

'That's it, everyone,' Fern called. 'I will put the cast list up on the Telling Tree after supper tonight so you'll be able to find out which part you have.'

Willow hardly ate any tea. Her stomach felt like it was going round and round with excitement. Who would be Sleeping Beauty? *I was better than Cadence, I'm sure I was,* she thought. *Oh, I hope I get the part!*

'Aren't you going to eat that?' Storm asked, looking at Willow's untouched food.

'I'm not very hungry,' she replied.

'Well, I'm starving,' said Storm, tucking in. 'I've been at my first extra transformation class this afternoon.'

'How was it?' Troy asked.

'Really good,' Storm replied. 'We were practising transforming leaves into brambles. In fact,' he added, looking down shyly, 'I managed to transform the most and Tor has asked me to be in charge of magicking the scenery for the enchanted forest.'

'Oh, wow!' Sapphire said. 'That's a really important piece of scenery.'

Storm nodded. 'I thought one of the older unicorns would get to do it.'

'But Tor asked *you*.' Willow nudged him. 'That's great, Storm!'

'I had good news today too,' said Troy, looking up from his feed bowl. 'There's going to be a flying display before the play at the end of term and I've been asked if I want to be in it.'

'Cool!' said Willow.

'I really hope we get good parts in the play, Willow,' Sapphire said. 'Then we'll all have fun things to do.'

Willow gave up on her food. 'I can't wait any longer. Let's go to the Telling Tree and see if the cast list is up yet.'

Willow and Sapphire weren't the only ones who had given up on their tea. Most of the unicorns who had auditioned were already heading over to the Assembly Fields. Willow's heart beat faster as she followed them. As she got near to the tree, Willow saw a piece of paper pinned to its trunk. 'The list's there!' she gasped.

She and the other unicorns all broke into a canter. Sapphire reached the tree just a few seconds

before Willow and pushed to the front.

'I'm the Prince!' Oriel neighed.

Willow heard Sapphire give an astonished whinny.

'What is it? Which part have you got?' Willow demanded.

Sapphire turned, her dark eyes wide. 'I . . . I'm Sleeping Beauty!'

Chapter Five

The Wicked Fairy

There was a roaring noise in Willow's ears and blood seemed to rush into her head. Willow stared at Sapphire. She couldn't be Sleeping Beauty. She just couldn't!

'Hey, well done, Willow,' Oriel said, swinging round. 'You're the

Wicked Fairy and that's one of the biggest parts.'

Willow pushed her way through the crowd. The list fluttered on the tree before her.

Sleeping Beauty . . . Sapphire
The Wicked Fairy . . . Willow
The Prince . . . Oriel
The King . . . Apollo
The Queen . . . Pearl
The Fairy Godmothers:
Cadence, Topaz, Sorrel,
Coral, Melody, Amethyst,
Meadowflax and Solitaire.

Disappointment swelled through Willow. She didn't want to be the horrible Wicked Fairy! She hadn't even auditioned for her. She'd wanted to be the beautiful princess. She wanted to wear a pink hat and sing a song and have everyone clap her. She backed away slowly from the tree trunk.

Sapphire was waiting at the edge of the crowd. Her eyes were anxious. 'Um . . . well done for getting the part of the Wicked Fairy.'

Willow didn't know what to say. She felt like crying, but seeing the worried look on her friend's face, she knew she couldn't.

Swallowing her disappointment she forced a smile. 'Thanks,' she muttered. 'Well done for getting the

part of Sleeping Beauty. You'll . . .
you'll be great.' Her eyes prickled.
She quickly bent down to rub her
leg with her nose so that Sapphire
wouldn't see her tears.

'Do you mind that I'm Sleeping
Beauty?' Sapphire asked her. 'I mean,
I know you really wanted the part.'

Willow brushed her tears away and
straightened up. 'It's fine,' she lied.

Sapphire looked at her uncertainly.
'If it's not, I could always ask Fern if
you could be Sleeping Beauty
instead of me.'

'No,' Willow protested. 'Fern chose

you. Well done, Sapphire. I mean it. I'll really enjoy being the Wicked Fairy.'

Sapphire looked relieved. 'That's OK then. Come on, let's go and tell Troy and Storm!'

She cantered off. Willow followed much more slowly. She wasn't Sleeping Beauty. She thought of the letter she'd written to her parents. Now she would have to write again and tell them that she hadn't got the part. She was the Wicked Fairy instead. Her heart sank.

It was hard to watch everyone congratulating Sapphire that evening. Willow felt mean for not being happier for her friend but she had

wanted to be Sleeping Beauty so
much. She was very glad when it
was time for bed.

'Night, Willow,' Sapphire said from
her stall.

'Goodnight,' Willow replied, trying
to sound cheerful. She knew she
should be happy for Sapphire but it
was just so hard.

'I can't wait until rehearsals start,'
said Sapphire dreamily.

'Mmm,' Willow said, and lying

down on the soft cloud floor, she gave a sad sigh and closed her eyes.

The next afternoon, the cast had their first rehearsal. 'Here are your scripts,' Fern told them. 'I want you all to have learnt your words in two weeks' time.'

'We can practise together,' Sapphire whispered to Willow.

'And one other thing before we get started,' Fern went on. 'Just in case anyone with a main part is ill on the day of the performance I am going to choose unicorns to understudy the main parts. If you are an understudy, it means you must learn the lines of the part you are understudying as well as your other lines. Willow, I would like you to be the understudy for Sleeping Beauty. Apollo, you will understudy the Prince and, Sorrel, you will understudy the Wicked Fairy.'

Willow didn't know whether to be pleased or not. It would be fun to be an understudy but it would be hard to practise the part she had really wanted too.

Fern sent a shower of sparks into the sky with her horn. 'Right, everyone. Let's begin with Scene One!'

As the rehearsal went on, Willow felt her unhappiness begin to fade.

Fern asked them to stand onstage and told them where she wanted them to move as they read out their lines. Although Willow would rather have been Sleeping Beauty, it *was* fun being the Wicked Fairy. The first scene they rehearsed was the baby Sleeping Beauty's naming ceremony. The Wicked Fairy had not been invited and she was very cross. Willow had to fly on to the stage and then march about scaring everyone. She had lots of lines to say and she was allowed to do magic too. She banged her horn on the stage and shot black stars out of it.

'Brilliant!' Fern exclaimed as

Willow swept an arc of green smoke after her.

'On her sixteenth birthday,' Willow cried, 'she shall prick her muzzle on a spindle and die!'

'That was fantastic, Willow!' Fern enthused.

'You're a cool Wicked Fairy!' said Oriel admiringly as she flew off.

Willow felt pleased. Being the Wicked Fairy might not be as good as being Sleeping Beauty, but she was beginning to enjoy it.

Afterwards, she and Sapphire headed back to Moonlight Meadows.

Storm saw them and cantered over. 'How did your rehearsal go?'

'Really well,' said Sapphire.

'How about you?' Willow asked. She knew Storm had been out in Bramble Forest searching for magic acorns and leaves to make the trees and brambles for the play.

'Well,' said Storm, 'I found enough leaves to make the brambles but I haven't got many acorns to make

the trees. Everyone else who is making scenery was in the woods collecting acorns too and there just aren't many on the ground at this time of year. I've got almost enough to make the enchanted forest so long as I don't make many mistakes.'

Willow smiled at him. 'You won't. Your scenery will be the best.'

Storm grinned back. 'I hope so!'

Chapter Six

Storm Gets It Wrong

Over the next few weeks, the school buzzed with activity for the play. There were acting and singing rehearsals every day, the backstage teams were busy making the scenery and costumes, and the flying team were busy practising their display. Fern and Tor dashed around the school, organizing people, putting posters up and making sure everyone was learning their lines.

Willow and Sapphire practised together every second they could. Willow soon knew the whole script off by heart. However, Sapphire found it much harder to learn her lines, and as it got closer and closer to the performance, she got more and more nervous.

'I'm never going to remember what I have to say,' she told Willow. 'There's only a week to go until the performance and I keep getting things wrong.'

'You'll be fine,' Willow said confidently.

'No, I won't,' Sapphire fretted. 'I shouldn't be Sleeping Beauty. I'm not good enough.'

'Yes, you are,' Willow said.

'I'm not. I'm useless.'

'Don't be silly,' Willow told her. 'You're great, Sapphire. You really are.'

Just then, Emerald, one of the older unicorns in charge of the costumes, came flying over. 'Sapphire, could you come for a costume fitting now? We need to see if your wedding outfit is the right size.'

'OK,' Sapphire replied.

Willow felt a flash of jealousy as Sapphire cantered off with Emerald. She had taken a quick peek at the wedding outfit that morning when the costume team had been making it. It was beautiful – a jewel-encrusted veil held in place by a tiara that would fit over Sapphire's horn, and a long white train that was embroidered with pearls and tiny red rubies. *I wish I could wear it*, Willow thought.

She headed to the Assembly Fields where the scenery was being made.

She knew she would find Storm there. The scenery for the earlier scenes had all been made and now it was his turn to create the enchanted forest.

Storm was standing by the stage with Troy. There were acorns scattered round them, but instead of a mass of trees and brambles, Storm appeared to have magicked up clumps of bullrushes. Both Storm and Troy were looking worriedly at them.

'Hi, you two!' called Willow. She looked curiously at the bullrushes. 'What's going on?'

Storm sighed. 'I've been trying to make the trees for the enchanted forest but I keep getting the magic wrong and getting these instead.' He pointed with his horn at the rushes.

'Oh,' said Willow.

'I don't know what to do,' said Storm. 'I'm running out of magic acorns. I've got just enough to make the trees, but if I get it wrong many more times, the forest is going to be really small.'

Willow frowned. 'Can't you get more magic acorns?'

'I went into the woods this morning but I couldn't find any,' Storm told her. 'I've just got to get it right with the acorns I have left.'

'Try again,' Troy told him. 'Concentrate really hard this time.'

'OK.' Storm went over to a nearby acorn. He looked nervous. 'Here goes.' He shut his eyes tightly and reached down to touch the acorn with his horn. But suddenly he pulled back. 'No, I can't do it. What if I waste this acorn?'

'You have to try,' Willow told him.

'Go on!' Troy said.

Storm gulped and shut his eyes again. This time he did touch the acorn with his horn. There was a purple flash. Willow caught her breath.

There, in front of them, was a clump of bullrushes.

Willow and Troy looked at each other.

Storm opened his eyes. 'It's happened again,' he said in dismay. 'The trouble is, every time I try to think of a tree, I just keep worrying that it's going to turn out to be a clump of rushes; then I see the rushes in my mind and the next minute the magic has worked . . . What am I going to do? We can't have a forest of bullrushes!'

'You'd better ask Tor for help,' said Troy.

'But I want to do it on my own,' said Storm. 'Everyone else has done their scenery without help and they've made it look really amazing. Tor will think I'm useless if I ask for help.' He hung his head. 'But then I guess I *am* useless.'

Willow nuzzled him. 'Oh, Storm. You're not. Look, why don't you leave it for now and try again tomorrow? You're probably just tired.'

Storm sighed. 'OK. But I'd better get it right tomorrow. I'm running out of acorns fast!'

They headed back to the castle.

'So where's Sapphire?' Troy asked
Willow.

'At a costume fitting,' Willow
replied.

'Did she remember her lines
today?' Storm asked. 'She was really
nervous this morning.'

'Well, she did forget some,'
Willow said. 'The trouble is, the

more nervous she gets, the more she forgets them.' *And the more she moans about it*, she added to herself. Then she felt bad. She knew Sapphire didn't moan on purpose. She was just really worried about playing Sleeping Beauty but her constant worrying and talking about how useless she felt was beginning to get on Willow's nerves.

If I had the main part like her I'd be really happy, Willow thought.

'I hope Sapphire stops feeling so nervous soon and learns her lines,' said Troy.

'Yes,' agreed Storm. 'And I hope I manage to get my scenery sorted

out so that it looks really good.
There's only a week to go!'

Willow's stomach seemed to do a
flip. Just one week. That wasn't long
at all!

Arguments and Acorns

On the evening before the performance, Fern called a meeting in the Assembly Fields for all the unicorns in the play. The scenery was at one end of the field. As Willow joined the others, she looked at it. Storm had turned most of his acorns into bullrushes before

he had managed to get the magic
right. But by then he only had a
few acorns left and so there were
just eight trees in the enchanted
forest.

'The enchanted forest isn't very
impressive, is it?' she heard Apollo
say. 'I'd have thought there would
have been loads more trees than
that.'

'Yeah,' said Ruby. 'Me too. The rest of the scenery's really good but the forest is rubbish.'

'Tor should have got one of the older unicorns to do it,' said Cadence.

Willow felt awful for Storm. She knew he was feeling really down about his scenery. She wished she could help.

Fern went up on to the stage and began to speak. 'As you all know, tomorrow is the performance. The parents will be arriving after lunch and everyone will watch the flying display; then I will call you all to come and get ready and we will perform the play. I have a few

scenes I would like to rehearse now.
I need the King and Queen and the
fairy godmothers first. The rest of
you can go and practise your lines.
Willow, I won't be needing you this
evening.'

Sapphire and Willow headed off
together. 'What am I going to do?'
Sapphire fretted. 'I'm sure I'm going
to forget all my lines tomorrow.'

'You won't,' Willow told her.

'I bet I will.' Sapphire swished her
tail anxiously. 'I really wish I had
fewer lines to learn. Sometimes I
hate being Sleeping Beauty.'

Willow bit her tongue. Sapphire
didn't realize how lucky she was!

'Oh, Willow, you don't know how

awful it is, having the main part!'

Willow's temper snapped. 'If you hate it so much, why did you audition to be Sleeping Beauty in the first place?' she burst out. 'You're really lucky, Sapphire. I would *love* to be Sleeping Beauty but all you do is moan about it! If you don't want to do it, don't do it, but stop going on about it to me!'

Anger beating through her, Willow galloped off.

As she reached the entrance to the Assembly Fields she glanced over her shoulder. Sapphire was staring after her, a shocked, hurt look on her face. Willow carried on going. She was fed up with having to tell

Sapphire how good she was, fed up with having to listen to Sapphire saying she wished she wasn't Sleeping Beauty. It wasn't fair! Not when she would have loved the part!

Willow cantered into Moonlight Meadows. Storm was there. 'Are you OK?' he asked her.

'Yes!' she snapped. Seeing the surprise on his face, she sighed. 'No. Not really,' she admitted. 'I just had an argument with Sapphire. She was going on and on about not wanting to be Sleeping Beauty so I told her *not* to be Sleeping Beauty then.'

'She's just nervous,' said Storm.

'I know,' Willow said. 'But it's

really annoying me.' She had a horrible feeling that he was going to tell her she should go and say sorry, so she quickly changed the subject. 'How are you?'

'Not great,' Storm replied. 'Have you seen the forest? It's a complete disaster. There are hardly any trees. I know everyone's talking about it.'

Willow felt very sorry for him. 'How about you try and find some more acorns?' she said. 'After all, you know how to turn them into trees now. I could come with you and we could see if we can find any together.'

'It's no use. I've searched and searched,' said Storm.

'Well, let's go and search some more,' said Willow. She hated seeing him so down. 'Come on. We might as well see what we can find before it gets dark.'

'OK,' Storm said reluctantly. 'I suppose we might as well look.'

They set off together for Bramble Forest. The sun was just starting to set in the sky. For a moment, a picture of Sapphire flashed across Willow's mind. What was Sapphire doing now? She remembered how upset her best friend had looked.

Guilt prickled through her but she forced it away and concentrated on helping Storm.

They reached the trees. The light

was dim inside the forest and it wasn't easy to spot which were magic oak trees.

'Light,' Willow murmured and her horn started to glow and sparkle. In the light that flooded from it she noticed that a nearby oak tree had leaves with golden spots on it. 'Here's a magic oak!' she called to Storm. Bending her head down she began to nose through the leaves

with her muzzle, her horn casting a silvery light on the ground. Storm joined her, his horn glowing too, but although they looked and looked, they couldn't find any acorns.

'Let's go further in,' Willow urged.

They wandered further and further into the trees but they couldn't find a single acorn. 'We'll find some soon,' Willow kept saying encouragingly.

'It's no good,' said Storm at last. 'I'll just have to give up.'

Willow looked at his unhappy face. 'No, you won't!' she told him firmly. 'We *will* find some acorns. I know we will.'

Storm heaved a heavy sigh. 'We won't; it's useless even looking.'

'It isn't!' Willow insisted. She couldn't let him give up so easily – not when it clearly meant so much to him. 'I don't care how late we have to look, we're not going to bed until we find some acorns. OK?'

Storm looked at her for a moment. 'OK,' he smiled, a new note of determination in his voice.

'What we need is to find a magic oak tree that no one else has been near,' Willow said.

'I wonder if there are any magic oaks anywhere else in the school grounds,' replied Storm.

Willow gasped. 'Of course! That's it, Storm! We're looking in the wrong place. We should see if we can find a magic oak tree *outside* the woods.' Her eyes widened. 'And I know *just* where we should look!'

Willow saw a picture in her mind of a tree's branches tapping against a window, each leaf with a gold spot at its base. 'By the elves' mail room!' she said. 'Come on!'

Where Is Sapphire?

Willow and Storm cantered
out of the woods. The sun
had set now and it was getting dark.
All the other unicorns had gone
back to their stables for the night.

'We'd better be quick,' said Storm.
'We should be in our stable by now.'

Willow nodded. As they cantered

through the archway towards the castle, her sharp eyes spotted the oak tree. It was hidden in a cluster of four trees that grew just beside the castle wall. Its branches spread across the windows of the mail room. 'There it is!' she exclaimed.

'And look! There are loads of acorns!' said Storm, pushing the fallen leaves on the ground aside with his nose. He began to pick them up with his mouth and put them into the bag round his neck. 'Oh, wow!'

Willow quickly helped. 'These are perfect!'

'I'm going to be able to magic lots of trees after all!' said Storm.

'Thank you so much. I'd have given up if it wasn't for you, Willow. You're such a good friend.'

An uncomfortable feeling ran through Willow. *A good friend?* She hadn't really been that to Sapphire.

'You're always helping people,' Storm went on, looking earnestly at her. 'And you make people feel better when they're down.'

Willow swallowed. She hadn't made Sapphire feel better. She'd been horrible to her. Sapphire had been upset and nervous and Willow had shouted at her and cantered off. *I have to say sorry*, she realized.

'OK, this should do,' said Storm, once his bag was full. 'I'll get up early tomorrow and transform them into trees. Come on, let's get back to the stables before an elf or teacher spots us and we get into trouble.'

As soon as they got to the stable, Willow looked over the partition into Sapphire's stall. Sapphire was lying down with her eyes shut. 'Sapphire?' Willow whispered.

Sapphire's eyes seemed to close even more tightly.

'Sapphire?' Willow repeated. She was sure her friend wasn't asleep, but Sapphire didn't say anything.

'I'm sorry,' Willow whispered.

Still Sapphire didn't open her eyes.

Willow was just wondering what to do when there was a rap at the stable door and an elf looked in. 'Time to go to sleep now,' he said. 'No more talking, please.'

Willow sighed. She'd have to make up with Sapphire in the morning.

But when Willow woke up, Sapphire's stall was empty. Willow frowned. It wasn't like Sapphire to get up early. 'Where's Sapphire gone?' she said in surprise.

Storm looked over from the other side. 'I don't know, but I should get going if I want to make those trees. I'll start now and then have a break for breakfast.'

'And I'd better get ready for flying practice,' said Troy. 'See you later, Willow.'

'Bye,' Willow called distractedly as they left the stable. She set off to look for Sapphire and eventually found her in the meadows with Cadence and Topaz. They were practising a scene from the play.

Willow halted. She didn't want to barge in and start apologizing to

Sapphire in front of the others.

Sapphire saw her watching and quickly turned her back. She didn't look very happy, her neck was tense and high and she kept forgetting her lines.

'What's the matter, Sapphire?' Topaz said. 'You were much better than this yesterday.'

'I'm sorry. I'm sorry,' Sapphire mumbled, looking close to tears.

'Let's start the scene again,' Cadence sighed.

Feeling worried that she was putting Sapphire off, Willow decided to leave them to it. *I'll talk to Sapphire at breakfast time*, she thought.

But Sapphire didn't turn up at

breakfast. When Willow asked Cadence where she was, Cadence shrugged. 'I don't know. She's probably just gone to practise her lines. I don't feel much like eating, either. I'm so nervous about the performance.'

Willow looked out for Sapphire after breakfast but she didn't appear, and when Sapphire wasn't there again at lunchtime, Willow began to get worried.

'I haven't seen Sapphire all morning,' she said to Storm and Troy.

'Me neither,' said Storm. 'But then I've just been in the Assembly Fields making trees.'

'How's it going?' Troy asked him.

'Really well!' Storm replied. 'I've made a whole forest!'

'That's brilliant, Storm,' Willow said, really pleased for him.

'I wonder where Sapphire is,' Storm said. 'Do you think we should go and look for her after lunch?'

Troy looked anxious. 'I won't be able to. I've got to get ready for the flying display as soon as I've finished.'

'It's all right,' Willow said. 'Storm and I will go.' Storm nodded, but as they tried to leave the table later on, Tor stopped them.

'No going off, you two!' he told

them. 'Everyone has to go to the Assembly Fields straight after lunch for the flying display.'

'But . . .' Willow broke off. She'd been about to explain about looking for Sapphire but she didn't want to get Sapphire into trouble for missing lunch.

Storm nuzzled her. 'Don't worry, Willow,' he whispered. 'I bet Sapphire's just been practising her lines and she will be in the Assembly Fields when we get there.'

Willow hoped he was right.

Ten minutes later, Tor led all the unicorns into the Assembly Fields.

Willow scanned the crowd, but although there were lots of parents all standing in rows, there was no sign of Sapphire. 'She's not here!' she hissed to Storm.

'And the display's about to start,' said Storm.

Just then the music for the display started up. Willow fidgeted anxiously. Oh, where was Sapphire? Why wasn't she there?

The flying display was very exciting with the team of twelve unicorns turning loop-the-loops and diving towards the ground before pulling up sharply and flying away.

Willow cheered as loudly as all the other watching unicorns but she couldn't really enjoy it. She was too worried about Sapphire.

Afterwards, along with the whole of the flying team, Troy bowed proudly, and then Fern stepped forward. 'There will now be a short break. Unicorns who are in the play, please could you come and get ready!'

'Storm, we've got to do something!' Willow said urgently as she and Storm followed the other unicorns who were involved in the play.

'I know,' Storm replied. 'We'd better go and look for her.'

But just then, Tor came over. 'Can
you come with me, please, Storm?
We need to set up the scenery.'

'But . . .' Storm began.

'Come on!' Tor said, trotting away.
'There's lots to do.'

Shooting Willow a helpless look,
Storm had to hurry after Tor.

Willow's heart sank. *It's down to me
to find her*, she thought.

She slipped away from the others. As soon as she was out of the Assembly Fields, she flew into the air. It was quicker to fly than to canter and she would get a better view of the school grounds. Where could Sapphire be? There was no sign of her in Moonlight Meadows or the Charm Fields. Willow flew on. She tried the Flying Heath and then the beach, but Sapphire wasn't anywhere to be found. Willow's heart pounded. Where *was* she?

She was about to fly back to the stables when suddenly her eyes fell on a half-hidden entrance to a cave in the Rose Quartz Cliffs on the beach. Sapphire loved the cave; it had glittering walls of rose quartz and it always seemed to gleam with a pink light.

Maybe she's in there, thought Willow. She hurried over and peered round the rock that half hid the entrance. 'Sapphire?'

She heard an intake of breath. Someone *was* there!

Willow squeezed quickly into the cave. Sapphire was standing near the back.

'What are you doing here?' Willow demanded.

'Go away,' Sapphire muttered, turning her back on Willow.

'But . . .'

'Leave me alone!' Sapphire's voice rose. 'I'm not coming out.'

'But you've got to!' Willow protested. 'All the parents are here. You've got to get ready for the play!'

'No, I haven't,' Sapphire muttered. 'I'm not doing it.'

Willow gasped. 'What?'

'I can't!' Sapphire swung round to face her. 'You were right. I should never have auditioned for the part of Sleeping Beauty.'

'Oh, Sapphire,' Willow said, going over and trying to nuzzle her. 'I'm really sorry I said that. I didn't mean it. Don't be silly.'

But Sapphire shied away. 'I'm not

being silly.' Tears muffled her voice.
'I can't be Sleeping Beauty. I'm not
good enough. You'll have to do it
instead.'

'Me?' Willow exclaimed.

Sapphire nodded. 'You're the
understudy. You know the lines even
better than I do. You do it.'

'But . . . but . . .'

'I mean it, Willow. I'll pretend to
be sick and you can play the part.'

Willow stared at her friend, her

thoughts racing. She could actually be Sleeping Beauty? It was what she had wanted. What she'd been longing for . . .

She saw a tear fall from Sapphire's eyes.

'But don't *you* want to be Sleeping Beauty?' Willow said slowly.

'Yes,' Sapphire said in a small voice, turning away. 'I'd love to but I'm not good enough.'

Looking at her friend's sad face, Willow suddenly knew what she had to do. Yes, she wanted to be Sleeping Beauty, but not if it meant Sapphire being unhappy.

'You *are* good enough,' she told Sapphire softly. 'Your acting and singing are brilliant and I know you'll remember your lines.' She touched her horn to Sapphire's neck. She had to make her friend believe her. 'You *can* do it, Sapphire.'

Willow's horn started to sparkle. Willow caught her breath in surprise — something magic was happening!

Sapphire wasn't looking at Willow and she hadn't noticed that Willow's horn was glowing. 'I *can* do it,' she whispered, half to herself. Her voice rose and became more determined. 'Yes, I really think I can.'

Willow felt a rush of delight. 'You'll be Sleeping Beauty?'

Sapphire nodded. 'I feel different —

braver, stronger. Just a moment ago I was sure I couldn't play the part but now . . .' She looked round at Willow and broke off. 'Willow!' she gasped. 'Your horn! It's glowing!'

'I know. Some sort of magic must be happening,' said Willow.

'Courage magic!' exclaimed Sapphire. 'I bet that's what it is. My dad told me about it. Unicorns can use their horns to make others feel braver. That's why I suddenly feel so much better. Oh, thank you, Willow!'

Willow felt a bit uncomfortable at accepting Sapphire's thanks. 'I didn't mean to do it. It just happened. I wanted to try and make you believe

how good you'd be as Sleeping
Beauty and then suddenly my horn
started shining.'

'Well, I don't care whether you
meant it or not. You're brilliant!'
Sapphire told her. 'You did magic
without even really trying *and*
you've made me realize that I can
be Sleeping Beauty in the play!'

'I wish I hadn't got cross with
you.' Willow nuzzled her friend. 'I
really am sorry, Sapphire. I shouldn't
have snapped.'

Sapphire nuzzled Willow back.
'That's OK. I guess I was being a
bit annoying and now you've made
me feel so much better.'

Willow felt a happy glow spread

through her. She knew she'd done
the right thing by making Sapphire
feel brave enough to be Sleeping
Beauty. There were some things far
more important than having the
main part.

Suddenly she realized that time
was passing. 'We'd better get a move
on,' she said. 'If we don't get back in
time, the play won't be able to start.'

Sapphire grinned at her. '*Sleeping
Beauty*, here we come!'

Chapter Nine

Sleeping Beauty

Willow and Sapphire raced to the Assembly Fields. Fern was bustling about backstage. She stared at them. 'Willow! Sapphire! Why aren't you in your costumes?'

'We're just getting them,' Willow said quickly.

They cantered to where the

costumes were kept and quickly got dressed. Two elves bustled around, helping them with their cloaks and hats.

Willow and Sapphire went to the side of the stage in their costumes. Willow had a grey cloak that looked like it had been made out of cobwebs, a black hat and black wispy material tied round her hooves. Sapphire had a pink cloak and a tall, pale pink hat that covered her horn. Looking at her, Willow realized that she didn't feel jealous. She stamped her front hooves. She was looking forward to going onstage and being the Wicked Fairy – to making silver stars and green smoke appear and to flying around scaring everyone.

'Beginners to stage, please. Beginners to stage!' Fern whinnied.

On either side of the stage, big curtains had been hung up so the audience couldn't see the cast. The stage itself was hidden by a deep red curtain trimmed with gold. On the other side of it, they could hear the chatter of the audience.

'It's scary! All our parents will be out there!' Sapphire whispered as she and Willow stood at the side of the stage.

'I can't believe it's the end of term and they're going to be taking us home afterwards,' said Willow. 'I'm really going to miss you in the holidays.'

'I'll miss you too,' Sapphire told her. 'But we can write and we'll only be at home for two weeks before we're back for next term.'

Willow nodded. 'Write to me every day!'

'I promise,' said Sapphire.

Just then Storm came over. 'Good luck, guys.'

'Thanks,' they chorused.

'The enchanted forest looks brilliant,' Sapphire told him. She and Willow had peeped at it as soon as they were in their costumes.

'Yeah, Storm,' said Apollo, who was passing. 'It's really cool. It looks loads better than it did yesterday.'

'I think it's the best bit of scenery,' said Ruby.

'Me too,' said Cadence.

Storm blushed but looked very pleased.

'Quiet, please!' called Fern. 'We're about to start. Stand by, everyone!'

'Oh, Willow, I'm so nervous!' Sapphire whispered.

'Don't worry,' Willow whispered back as the curtains started to open. 'You're going to be brilliant!'

The lights went off. Willow took a deep breath. This was it! She was the first unicorn who had to go onstage.

'Good luck!' Willow felt Sapphire's muzzle touch her shoulder and then there was a loud bang like a thunderclap. The play was starting!

With a loud whinny, Willow galloped on to the stage. She sent a jet of green smoke out of her horn and stopped dead. The lights came on and Willow reared up. 'I am the

Wicked Fairy!' she declared. There were some boos and hisses from the audience. Willow cackled and sent up a flurry of silver stars that spelt out her name: *WICKED FAIRY*. The boos and hisses got louder.

'Be quiet, you horrible rabble!' Willow pranced about the stage looking as cross and as frightening as she could, but inside she was

grinning in delight. This was really fun!

Scene after scene flew by. When it came to Sapphire's first entrance she looked really scared. She got onstage and opened her mouth but no words came out.

'Today's my sixteenth birthday,' Willow hissed from the side of the stage.

Sapphire sent her a grateful look. 'Today's my sixteenth birthday,' she said to the audience. 'I wonder what I will do. I think I might go exploring.'

After that, Sapphire remembered all her lines and she sang her songs beautifully.

Willow had a great time, going onstage and doing her magic. At one point she even flew over the audience's head, sending stars shooting down at them. The audience applauded loudly.

'Next time, I'll turn you all into frogs . . . or maggots! Ha!' cried Willow, flicking her mane. Turning a somersault in the air, she flew off the stage.

'Brilliant!' Fern exclaimed.

At last it was time for the big finale – the wedding scene. All the unicorns apart from Willow went onstage. She was left out because the Wicked Fairy hadn't been asked to the wedding. The unicorns stood in two lines and made a corridor with their horns touching. Sapphire and Oriel came onstage in their glittering wedding outfits. They walked through the archway of horns and stopped at the front of the stage. The audience cheered and stamped their hooves as Sapphire and Oriel bowed. Then the other unicorns bowed too.

Willow felt slightly lonely waiting by herself offstage but she knew that in a minute all the cast would get into a line for a final bow and she would go on then. Or at least that was what was supposed to happen, but just then someone shouted, 'We want the Wicked Fairy!'

And then another voice echoed
the shout, 'We want the Wicked
Fairy!'

More and more of the audience
began to join in until it seemed
like everyone out there was chanting
the words, 'We want the Wicked
Fairy!'

Willow looked at Fern, wondering
what she should do.

'You'd better go onstage, Willow,' Fern said, grinning. 'Go on!'

'But . . . but . . . it isn't the right time yet,' Willow protested.

'The audience seems to think it is!' said Fern. 'And that's all that matters.' She nudged Willow on to the stage. For a moment, Willow stood there feeling almost embarrassed but then the audience broke into loud cheers and her awkwardness faded away. The lights shone down on her and she cantered to the centre of the stage. Oriel and Sapphire parted and made room for her. The three of them bowed together and the audience stamped their hooves as loudly as they could.

Oriel and Sapphire took a step back and Willow bowed on her own. She felt like she was glowing with happiness. The audience had liked her – really liked her. *I guess I was right. Having the main part isn't that important after all*, she realized, as she stepped back into line, the cheers ringing in her ears.

After the final bows had been taken and everyone had changed out of costume they all went to meet their parents in Moonlight Meadows.

Willow spotted her parents standing by the food table. 'Mum! Dad!' she cried.

She cantered over. Her mum gave
a delighted whinny and stepped
forward to greet her. As she and
Willow nuzzled each other's faces,
Willow caught her dad's eye.

'We're so proud of you,' he told
her. Willow felt as if she was about
to burst with joy.

Sapphire trotted by. 'Sapphire!'
Willow exclaimed. 'Come and meet
my mum and dad!'

'Hi,' Sapphire said, smiling at them.

Suddenly there was the sound of a
horn blowing and everyone fell
silent as the Tricorn walked into the
meadows.

'Welcome, everyone,' he said. 'I
hope you all enjoyed the production.

The cast put on a fantastic show. We had a beautiful Sleeping Beauty, a brave Prince, some wonderful flying from the fairy godmothers, and the most wicked of all wicked fairies!'

The unicorns stamped their hooves.

'Sapphire,' the Tricorn said, when the noise quietened, 'you had the main part; would you say a few words to everyone?'

Sapphire's eyes widened. She took a deep breath. 'Um . . . well, I'd like to thank everyone for coming and watching. We all had great fun doing it. Fern and Tor have been brilliant and everyone's worked really hard.

Not just the cast but the people backstage too.'

Storm caught Willow's eye and grinned.

'That's all I've got to say, really,' said Sapphire. 'Apart from one other thing. I'd like to thank Willow, who was the Wicked Fairy. I was almost too frightened to go onstage but she made me realize I could do it. Thank you, Willow,' Sapphire said, looking at her. 'I wouldn't have been Sleeping Beauty without you. You're the best friend anyone could ever have.'

Storm stepped forward. 'And I couldn't have made the enchanted forest without Willow either,' he

announced loudly. 'She really
helped me when I was about to
give up.'

Everyone cheered loudly and
stamped their hooves some more.
Willow didn't think she'd ever felt
happier.

The Tricorn whinnied and silence

fell. 'It is the end of the school term today,' he said. 'It has been a full and busy time and much has been learnt.' His eyes twinkled. 'Have a good journey home, everyone, and we will see you in two weeks!' He tossed his head up and a stream of gold, silver and bronze stars cascaded out of his multicoloured horn. They exploded with a bang over the watching unicorns and rained down sparkly dust.

The horn was blown again and the Tricorn left the meadows.

Willow turned to Sapphire. 'Thank you for saying that about me,' she said softly.

'It's the truth,' Sapphire said.

'Come on, Willow. Time to go home,' said her dad.

'Bye, Sapphire!' Willow said.

'Bye, Willow!' Sapphire replied. 'I'll write every day!'

Willow saw Storm and Troy by the food table. 'Just a minute,' she said to her mum and dad. She cantered over. 'Bye, you two. I've got to go.'

'Have a good holiday, Willow,' said Storm.

'Yeah,' said Troy. 'See you next term.'

'Come on, Willow!' her mum called.

Willow swooped into the air. The sun was setting and the golden

light glinted on her horn. She felt
very happy. She was looking
forward to going home but she was
also looking forward to coming
back to school in a few weeks'
time.

What's next term going to be like?
she wondered.

She didn't know, but one thing
was certain – she couldn't wait to
find out!

Discover magical new worlds with
Linda Chapman